Little Red Riding Hood

Little Red Riding Hood

A STORY BY THE BROTHERS GRIMM

WITH PICTURES BY HARRIET PINCUS

A Voyager Book
Harcourt Brace Jovanovich, Inc., New York

illustrated by Harriet Pincus
(available in hard-cover editions)

THE WEDDING PROCESSION OF THE RAG DOLL AND THE BROOM HANDLE AND WHO WAS IN IT by Carl Sandburg

TIT FOR TAT: And Other Latvian Folk Tales retold by Mae Durham

WHO IS PADDY? by Elizabeth K. Cooper

LITTLE RED RIDING HOOD by the Brothers Grimm

ISBN 0-15-652850-9
Library of Congress Catalog Card Number: 68-11505
Printed in the United States of America
A B C D E F G H I J

For Steve

Once upon a time there was a sweet little maid who was loved by everyone who knew her. She was especially dear to her grandmother, who never tired of doing things for her. Once she made her a little hood of red velvet, which was so becoming that she never wore anything else. After that, people always called her Little Red Riding Hood.

One day her mother said to her, "Little Red Riding Hood, here are some cakes and a jar of honey for you to take to Grandmother. She is weak and ill, and they will do her good. Go at once before it grows hot, and walk properly and nicely. If you run, you may fall and break the jar of honey, and then there would be none left for Grandmother. And when you go

into her room, don't forget to say, 'Good morning,' and ask how she feels."

"I will be very careful," Little Red Riding Hood promised her mother.

Now her grandmother lived deep in the woods, half an hour's walk from the village, and when Little Red Riding Hood reached the woods, she met a wolf. Since she did not know how wicked he was, she did not feel frightened.

"Good day, Little Red Riding Hood," said he. "Where are you going to so early?"

"To my grandmother's," she answered politely.

"And what are you carrying in your basket?"
"Cakes and honey. My grandmother is very weak and ill, and they will do her good."

"Where does your grandmother live, Little Red Riding Hood?"

"Her house stands beneath three tall oaks, near a grove of hazelnut trees," replied Little Red Riding Hood.

The wolf thought to himself, "This tender young thing would be a delicious meal and would taste even better than the old one. I must manage somehow to get both of them."

Then he walked along with Little Red Riding Hood for a while, thinking hard, and at last he said, "Little Red Riding Hood, look at the pretty flowers growing all around you. Don't hurry so. You should enjoy them. You are not even listening to the songs of the birds, though they're so delightful here in the woods."

Little Red Riding Hood walked more slowly and looked around her, and when she saw the lovely flowers everywhere, she thought to herself, "If I take a pretty nosegay to my grandmother, she will be very pleased, and there is plenty of time."

So off she ran. For each flower she picked, she saw a still prettier one beyond, and so she went farther and farther from the path. But the wicked wolf went straight to Grandmother's house and knocked at the door.

"'Who is there?" cried the grandmother.

"Little Red Riding Hood," he answered in as gentle a voice as possible, "and I have brought you some cakes and honey. Please open the door."

"Lift the latch," cried the grandmother. "I am too weak to get up."

The wolf lifted the latch, the door flew open, and he fell on the grandmother and swallowed her whole. Then he put on her clothes and her nightcap, lay down in her bed, and drew the curtains.

All this time Little Red Riding Hood was gathering flowers, and when she had as many as she could hold, she set off once more for her grandmother's.

She was surprised to find the door standing open, and when she went inside, she felt very strange.

"Oh dear, how frightened I am, though I don't know why! And I was so happy this morning to be coming to Grandmother's!"

When she said, "Good morning," there was no answer. Then she went up to the bed and drew back the curtains. There lay her grandmother with her cap pulled over her eyes, so that she looked very odd.

"Oh, Grandmother, what big ears you have!"
"The better to hear you with, my dear!"

"Oh, Grandmother, what big eyes you have!"
"The better to see you with, my dear."
"Oh, Grandmother, what big hands you have!"
"The better to hold you with, my dear."

"But, Grandmother, what big teeth you have!"
"The better to eat you with, my dear!"

And no sooner had the wolf said this than he bounded out of bed and swallowed up poor Little Red Riding Hood in one

gulp. Having satisfied his hunger, he lay down again in bed, fell asleep, and began to snore loudly.

A huntsman who was passing by the house heard him and thought, "How the old woman snores—I had better see if there is anything the matter with her."

So he went into the room and walked up to the bed, and there was the wolf lying fast asleep.

"At last I have found you, you old sinner!" said he. "I have been looking for you for a long time!"

Just as he was about to shoot the wolf, he thought, "Perhaps he has swallowed the grandmother whole and she may yet be saved!" So he did not fire, but took a big pair of scissors and began to cut the wolf's stomach. When he had made a few snips, Little Red Riding Hood appeared, and after a few more snips she jumped out and cried, "Oh, how frightened I have been! It is so dark inside the wolf."

And then out came the old grandmother, still living and breathing.

Little Red Riding Hood went quickly and fetched some large stones with which she filled the wolf's body, and her grandmother sewed him up.

When he woke up and was going to run away, the stones were so heavy that he fell down dead.

All three of them were very happy. The huntsman took the wolf's skin and carried it home. The grandmother ate the cakes and honey and felt much better, and Little Red Riding Hood said to herself that she would never again wander alone in the woods, but would always mind what her mother had told her.